Dutch~Henry

Written & Illustrated

By edwin gilven ©

All Rights Reserved

ISBN: 978-1-365-84063-0

ISBN: 978-1-365-84063-0

Foreword

Dutch-Henry is the second of a three book trilogy concerning coming of age. Dutch-Henry; young and determined to fulfill his burning desire all young rabbits have. 'To Come of Age' ~ to be an adult! And on this quest, Dutch-Henry will soon discover coming of age is much more than high dreams and heroic deeds!

Hop alongside him as he heads South to fulfill his quest ~ Bring yourself a lunch; it could be a long journey!

Acknowledgement

I would like to take this time to thank my brother Ron Gilven and his family, my sister Phyllis Gilven Enzor, Richard Jones and family, my sister-in-law Simone Tate & family, Sister Filmore & family, Mrs. Melvinnie Christian, Larry Marks, Ken & Tina Krick and staff. Michelle Bentz and family, My boyz at Last Stop Computer, Goodfellas Barbershop, Tami Elliott (My Citizen), Teri Lowe Dodge (Firefighter Extraordinaire), Sharon Lacey (Comedian), DeanneMichelle', Sabrina Nowell and her family, Stan (the man) Skinner, Marco Cabañas, Brandi Westernhausen, Mr. Hunter & wife Virginia owners of Tuff T's, My neighbors on East 64th Street, 98404. The families of; Willee Shenkel, Kenny & Michael Bush, Curtis Dahlgren, Jim Riley (Bodeen), Ralph Tipton, Tyler Johnson, Gary Pisani, Ron & Teresa Kelly, Varrice Spice, Eddie Gales. Thomas Barr. And wonderful Gail, Dixie and Teresa my Kent, WA ladies!

My friends from a far; Floyd Hall, Sr. & family, Nathanial (Lamont) Thompson, and Mr. John Robinson and his wife, Janice; I must also thank my Higher Power, and *so many others for their supportive love and rich encouragement.* Their never-ending belief in my work has been a great inspiration. For without their daily persistence this book would have not been possible ~ much love and respect to you all! And **sooooooo many more!**

A Special Dedication to my parents, Mr. & Mrs. Gilven, who are now long gone from this world, Love you, both!   -

Again, I thank you all!

edwin ~

Chapter 1

DUTCH-HENRY

It was in the year when Dutch-Henry believed he had come to age and somehow knew his destiny lied in the Deep South some thousand miles away. Dutch-Henry never realized that becoming of age was much more than high spirits and perfect dreams. You see, Dutch-Henry was nothing more than a small baby rabbit getting ready to face a world that was fairly new to him. Dutch-Henry, light-gray with a fluffy white chest, spoke,

"Mother, don't worry, I'll be alright. All rabbits go south to fulfill their destiny and so must I." His mother slowly pulled her apron sadly, "Son, you're just a baby, my oldest! This journey is too long for you, son!" In her heart she knew she was right, but Dutch-Henry had decided. His mother gave him a new blue backpack with food and other rabbit provisions then hugged him dearly. As she held onto him, he could see his little brothers and sisters busily playing, and tumbling over one another. They had no idea that their brother was about to leave them and perhaps never to return. He stared at them with a soft smile and waterier eyes. He waited for his mother to release him. When she did, he stepped back, adjusted his backpack straps and spoke softly, "I'll be back mom." He turned and scurried away from the securities of his home. As he dashed off, he could hear his mother shout.

"Watch out for the *'silent death!'* Watch out for the *'silent death'!"* Not wanting to show any emotions to his mother he continued to hop away.

Many hours later of hopping the noon sun was bright; Dutch-Henry began to talk aloud. "Whew! Never thought I would get so hungry. I'll just twist my backpack around to the front." *(All smart rabbits knew that survival sometimes meant eating on the road and to always keep moving).* After some difficulties getting his backpack to the front without stopping or dropping the bag; he unzipped one of the three pouches to pull out a sliced carrot. He looked at the neatly sliced carrot and jokingly laughed. "Ahahah, awe, my dearest mother." He smiled and bit into the carrot. *"CRUNCH!"*

DUST: It would soon be evening within the next hour or so and that was when Dutch-Henry passed a road tramp *(a wolf dressed in old and tattered clothing).* The tramp shouted to him!

"Boy, stop!! I won't harm you! Please help me!!" The wolf hobbled in front of Dutch-Henry in an effort to slow him down, but little Dutch-Henry casually sided hopped him and quickly scurried away. Miles down the road as he continued to hop he spoke aloud to himself. "Boy, I felt bad about not stopping for that old fellow. He did look down and out on his *luck*. But, mother always told me not to trust strangers." He looked back to see if he could see the wolf with an uneasiness in his heart for the unfortunate tramp; nevertheless it was almost night; time to find a quiet place to sleep. He had never slept alone before and never outside. Dutch-Henry built a small fire to keep warm. All was quiet as he ate very little and soon was fast asleep. It was much later into the night when he was rudely awakened by someone's hands. Hands that were choking him!! Immediately opened his eyes and -

"Fool, boy!!" It was the tramp! "I asked you to share with me! Help me! But, no-o-o! You closed your eyes to my needs!" The tattered clothed wolf squeezed Dutch-Henry's neck even hard! "*HA, HA, HAH!* Now, I'll take everything, including your life! *HA! HA! HA! HA-A-A-A!*" In frenzy to survive, Dutch-Henry clawed and scraped the ground to reach his backpack! He was getting dizzy! The wolf began to bang his head hard to the ground! When surprisingly, one of the squeezing hands slightly slipped, and that was more than enough for Dutch-Henry! He slipped his neck free! He hopped to left, then to the right as he grabbed his backpack! The wolf screamed, "Stop, you fool stop-p-p-p!" By this time little Dutch-Henry had scampered through the wolf's opened legs and dashed away from this disaster! His mother had warned him never to travel at night but, this time, the choice

wasn't his. The little rabbit ran and ran and ran! He finally stopped to rest safely behind a large bolder. While resting and breathing hard, through the darkness he saw four field mice searching the forest's floor for food. As he watched them busily search about, a huge shadow passed over him – He looked up and saw an owl of great size silently swoop down and grabbed one of the four mice! Frighten, he clumsily back into the huge bolder in terror *as* he shuddered knowing he'd just witnessed his first sight of death! It was so quick, so silent – *'the silent death'!* Dutch-Henry now knew what the silent death meant – Animals that flew! The little gray rabbit began to experience fear again! He looked quickly from side to side, then, he dashed down the first available path! As he curved down one of the many paths, he saw a little opening hid by some bushes. He slid to a stop, back peddled and ran into opening! There he camouflaged the entrance. There he would be safe and there he would soon fall asleep from exhaustion.

Chapter 2

A NEW FRIEND

Morning came early and Dutch-Henry still remembered last night. He slowly poked his head from the safety of his camouflaged cave. All was clear, he tightened the straps to his blue backpack; then, dashed away with great precaution. Once again, he had to eat on the run. This journey south was beginning to get more hazardous than expected.

It was on a hazy morning six days later, when little Dutch-Henry came to an open meadow that had a fence partly torn down at the far side of the field. The sun was due to break through the clouds and only then would he cross this open field. "I won't cross that field without the sun to cast shadows about. It wouldn't be wise; nor would it be safe; nooo-o, not me, buddie." He quietly lied down and waited. Hours passed and no bright sun broke through the clouds. Time was slipping away. Dutch-Henry slowly took a deep breath, "Oh, boy, it look like there will be no bright sunshine this day. I'll have to hop across this huge field with stopping." He disappointingly sighed as he shook his head. Then off and hopping did he go. This meadow would take approximately 10 to 15 minutes to cross without stopping. Such a huge task he thought; *'But, I must do it because it is so necessary to do'*. And as usually, Dutch-Henry ate on the run. His blue backpack was now in front in its familiar eating position.

After several minutes of traveling, he was halfway across the field when he felt something bite him on his back shoulder. "Umph!! A flea is biting me on my shoulder. Umph! I can't  stop to get it off either. Not in this open field. I'm almost to the other side though." The closer Dutch-Henry got to the broken fence, the more the itch persisted! He hopped only a few yards further when he yelled in frustration and agony! "Ar-gh-hh! This itch!!!!!, Ar-ghhh!"

He had stopped 20 yards short of the fence when;

he reached over his left shoulder to scratch this relentless itch and saw two sharp talons swooping down toward him! No time to run as he turned to face sure death. The pair of sharp claws ripped into his backpack! The talon's belonged to a red hawk! The impact sent him tumbling backward toward to the ground! The rabbit quickly rolled to his feet and charged toward the forest! The hawk by this time had circled up and was coming back to strike again! Dutch-Henry knew what was flying down at him, the Silent Death! He also knew that he had to make it to the fence and into the woods for survival. He gallop hopped as fast as he could as the red hawk was gaining on him. Near the fence he used all the muscles in his legs and took one large hop that landed him near the broken fence! He bounced and slid under the fence as dirt and small peddles flew wildly in all directions! Dutch-Henry had slid off a short slope and went tumbling down; meanwhile the red hawk had to dodge tree branches in her way. The hawk screamed in disgust! *"QUARK-K-K-K!"*

Sliding down the small slope with dirt and rocks following him, the rabbit tumbled to a stop nose to nose to a frog. *(Mordecia, the Amazing*).* "I see that you've met Lady Red?" He casually continued. "She sometimes can be a real nuisance." He pointed to Dutch-Henry's torn

* See *"Mirabella"*, by Edwin Gilven   11

backpack which dangled to one side of his chest. "Better fix that before you lose it." Dutch-Henry still in a state of shock looked down at backpack, "You, you, know that 'silent death'? Why was she after me?! Look at my bag! Look at me! I'm, I'm, I, I. . ."

"Whoa-a, slow down little fellow, it is survival – you see, Lady Red must survive and to survive, one must eat. The lady have nothing against you, it was just business." Mordecia smiled as he watched the red hawk fly away high in the sky.

"Huh, some kinda business she runs. Well, she can just leave me out of her business." Dutch-Henry too, also watched the red hawk fly away from their eyesight.

That evening the two become friends and by the next morning Dutch-Henry found his ability to laugh return through smiles that friendly conversation and companionship can bring. Plus, to his delight, Mordecia was also headed south. There was such a joy he felt learning from this knowledgeable frog; there was no comparison in learning. Day and night they travel, and soon their time together turned in months. And it was on the wettest day of their journey when Mordecia stopped.

"Well, Dutch-Henry, this is where our paths' part. My road leads to the right. Yours goes left. Your fur has turned white and with all of this snow on the ground you should be fairly safe." He shrugged his tiny shoulders and continued. "That is if all of this rain doesn't melt it way." Water dripped from his small body as he slowly turned away from the rabbit. Dutch-Henry by now had grown in size and had better control of his emotions than previous times took a deep breath ~ "How can I thank you, Mordecia? You have taught me so much. I can never re-pay you."

"Sure you can. Just stay alive." Then he smiled as the two friends high-fived one another with laughter *(slapping hands with another up high)*. They both bounced away from each other with joy and sadness. "Be safe, Dutch-Henry." Then, Mordecia, the Amazing Frog and young Dutch-Henry went their separate way.

Unexpectedly, Mordecia shouted back at the young rabbit. "Hey, Dutchie, if you ever need me – look me up in Spiritville." Dutch-Henry adjusted his backpack's scraps as he watched his new friend cheerfully hop away into the wet white forest as the rain continued to fall.

"Good-bye friend," whispered the rabbit. "I've learn well." Then he too turned and continued his way south. This particular morning really wasn't been a good one. Rain and snow, snow, and rain; his white fur was soaked.

He finally had to find a secure place to rest. It would soon be time to eat. And he could hardly wait to eat. Hours later after finding just the right hole in the ground to rest, he stumbled upon a nightmare . . . A wolverine! He gasped,

Mordecia had explained to him about the many dangerous predators throughout these woods and wolverines were definitely were businessmen of survival – They were known to chase a prey until it collapsed from exhaustion. The young rabbit slowly ducked low so that he wouldn't be seen. It made no sense in crawling into this small hole now. The wolverine would just tear it open.

Dutch-Henry lied motionless. But his nightmare became real because the large animal rose into the air and ~

"Hey, you stop! I want you!" There was no grace about his hunting method! The wolverine snarled viciously as he quickly dropped down and loped toward Dutch-Henry in gigantic bounds! Dutch-Henry knew his fate – but, he also knew his abilities – and the survival chase was on!

As the wolverine closed the gap between the rabbit he lunged only to miss! He circled back slipping and sliding in the slushy snow! He hissed and snared as the rabbit furiously fast hopped passed him toward the muddy forest as the rain continued to melt the snow! Dutch-Henry fighting his fears remembered that Mordecia had mentioned that there's no fear greater than the fear from within – *I must, I must think!!* Dutch-Henry slid to a stop, the wolverine slid pass him – but not before slashing a huge claw at the rabbit's legs! High into the air hopped Dutch-Henry over the swooping claw! *SWOOSH!* As the wolverine regained his balance he once again leaped at Dutch-Henry! nevertheless, the rabbit was able to squeeze through the wolverine's legs as he hopped toward a large bush he saw the a distance! There he could hide! – With amazing quickness, he made it! Here he would be safe. This little pause was more than enough rest for him. *WHAMMM!* Up side Dutch-Henry's head landed a hard blow! It staggered him out of the bush as he rolled and slid through the mud and slushy snow dirtying his white fur! No time to think only to move! As quick as he was, the wolverine once again landed inches away from clawing him! Dutch-Henry silently thanked Mordecia as he rolled to safety. He then saw a tall tree and ran toward it while the wolverine was confused as he slipped and slide on the slushy snow ~ the young rabbit dove behind the thin tree to shelter him from the wolverine, he took a deep breath, and sighed in relief – *CRASH-H-H!* The wolverine had smashed through the thin tree grabbing Dutch-Henry's backpack by the straps and sent the rabbit hurling backward! The wolverine went sliding on his face and loss his grip on the backpack and rabbit! Once again, precious time was granted. And once again it was accepted. Down the wet slushy field hopped and slid Dutch-Henry. The wolverine pushed the splintered wood aside as he continued the hunt! His looping style of running was so strange yet so affective because soon he had the rabbit in sight! As he closed the gap, Dutch-Henry slid to a halt and jumped onto a frozen little stream of water that slid down the side of a hill.

Down, down, down, slid the rabbit while his blue backpack served as a soft back cushion that increased his sliding speed that was so desperately needed! Meanwhile; the wolverine was right behind him. Dutch-Henry emerged from the small frozen stream onto a fairly large frozen lake! He spun a wide and large circle to a stop. After that, he had to hop over the diving wolverine that had already made up the distance between them! As Dutch-Henry touched down and began to run, his footing failed him! He slipped on the ice the same time the wolverine took a step toward him only to slip himself! They both fell at the same time! As Dutch-Henry frantically crawled away - all of a sudden, three white-furry weasels appeared! They slid onto the ice!

"Cousin, Wolv! We'll get him for ya!" As they quickly slid toward the spinning rabbit; (who was trying to stop!) they continued to shout, "Whoa-a, look a white rabbit with a blue backpack! Must be one of those Mid-westerners! Ha, hah!" Dutch-Henry never heard a word they said, he was too busy trying to hop backward! He quickly twisted and spun around in mid-air ~ SWOOSH! The wolverine was back on the attack! He wildly went sailing over the rabbit and bounced himself all the way across the frozen lake only to crash into his three cousins. Unfortunately, that was little or no problem for the weasels ~ they were so agile! They rolled with amazing quickness and was back on their feet chasing the rabbit! By now, Dutch-Henry had rested in the middle of the frozen lake. These gentlemen predators now knew the rabbit was trapped. Dutch-Henry breathing extremely hard and patiently watched as the weasel slowly moved toward him. The wolverine even now showed a sense of patience. He slowly rose to his hind legs and moved in closer with the pack – they all drooled saliva from their mouths. The snow had finally stopped, but the rain continued to fall ~ the weasels laughed and whinnied as they closed in for the feast. Hurriedly, all four predators leaped for the killed!

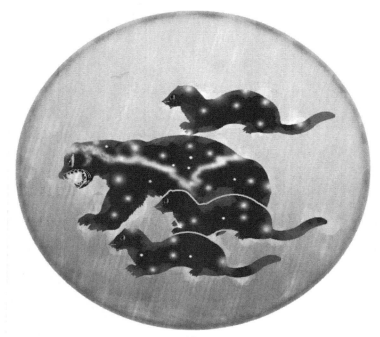

"Have to time this perfect..." thought, Dutch-Henry. As these businessmen flew toward him, Dutch-Henry gave it his all! He hopped tremendously high straight up into the air just barely over the crashing crowd below him! Having enough height; he lazily threw his arms up and did a slow backward somersault! The family of weasel crashed together onto the ice too hard and broke through the frozen lake at the same time Dutch-Henry landed safely away from the hole in the lake! As he slid backward on his hind legs he slipped and fell onto his chin. *BAM!* There, he continued his slide; he had to use his arms to balance himself to spin around; after that, he sprung onto the slushy white snow. He could hear yelling, screaming, and complaining from behind, but he never looked back as he hopped away and into the forest where he would be safe – and there he was safe.

Later that night, miles away from the lake and weasels, he finally pulled off his backpack to rest as he disappointedly touched his sore lips. "Look at this! My bag is badly torn! My lips are cut! (He sighed). I wonder if life is always so full." He reached into his bag for a carrot, but, discovered – "Oh, no-o-o! I lost all my food!" He threw his backpack down. Frustrated, he leaned back onto a tree stump and there he pouted!

The next couple of weeks were rather rough. Mordecia had told him how to find food. The food was scarce. He had never liked grass. Now he would eat grass and even the roots! Never facing hunger before was such a depressing experience and this made Dutch-Henry very disappointed.

Chapter 3

Steilwater Runs Deep

EARLY SUMMER: It was on another beautiful morning when Dutch-Henry had finally reached deep into the south. His fur had since changed back to its original color; light gray with a fluffy white chest. Frosted berries dangled freely from fat bushes everywhere. They looked so sweet, so bright. The very thought of tasting these juicy berries definitely tickled his tummy. Soon his backpack would be filled with little apples, nuts and *grass*. It was such a fun day for him and as the evening sun faded from the sky, his tired eyes slowly faded along with the dimming daylight.

The next day was extremely pretty – the sky was bright and blue, birds flew spiritedly high as he watched them sing their morning songs. He stood on a water dock that over looked a lagoon. "So, this is the place. My destination; my purpose for breathing these past months – What do I do now?" Then –

"Dutch-Henry?" someone yelled. "Are you Dutch-Henry?" Dutch-Henry slowly turned and saw another

rabbit. She wore a large pink ribbon tied around her neck.

She hopped closer and continued to speak. "I've been waiting for you. Mordecia told me to watch for you. I am Yolandor. I know why you've come so far and why you're here. It's lying at the bottom of this lagoon. It's a small box that you must bring to the surface to complete your growing that all rabbits must face." Dutch-Henry turned to the murky looking water. "I have to go into that water? Hummh, - well-l-l-l, I'll just go in and get this over with. Where is it down there?" He took off his backpack and gave it to Yolandor. She teasingly bowed her head – then lightly scratched the side of her forehead hesitantly,

"Ah-h-h, it's under a large rock." She paused, looked to the water; then, back at Dutch-Henry. "There's an alligator down there – and it's BIG! They call him Steilwater." Then she gave Dutch-Henry a big smile; "Can you swim?"

"Not that well. But I know a frog that can!" They simultaneously shouted - "Mordecia!"

Two days later, it was mid-afternoon – Mordecia, Yolandor, and Dutch-Henry stood over the lagoon. Mordecia stared at Dutch-Henry, "We need a distraction."

"Surely, you don't mean? I can't swim that well!" Dutch-Henry turned to Yolandor and saw the disappointment through her big brown eyes. He rolled his eyes to the sky, "Whew-w-w, alright, what can I do?"

"Just distract Steilwater for me a minute or two. You'll have to come of age. I can't do it alone."

Mordecia smiled. "I figure if you enter the lagoon at the far end, he'll see you and I can sneak behind him to get the box that he's guarding. He'll be too busy chasing you to see me." Dutch-Henry took a very long and slow deep breath. "You better be quick, because I won't be in the water that long." Mordecia smiled, "Ha, ha, neither will I – come on, let's get this over with." He turned to Yolandor - "Stay close by to help Dutch-Henry out of the water. He'll probably need your help." Dutch-Henry looked at them both. Loosen his backpack, but didn't take it off. "Well . . . let's go."

It took the frog several minutes to reach the other side of the lagoon. Once on the other side, he waved. Dutch Henry slowly entered the murky water. As soon as he and his blue backpack vanished into the water, Mordecia entered the lagoon himself. It was a little time later before Steilwater saw Dutch-Henry swimming down in his domain. He lay quietly-still and patiently waited for the rabbit to come closer, but, Dutch-Henry didn't, instead he started to swim up and toward the surface. You see, Dutch-Henry needed air! He began to panic in mind and body! *"I, I, I can't make it!! I'm going to drown! I'm not going to make it!"* His whole life began to flash and spin before him. He saw his little brothers and sisters playing. He saw the 'silent deaths', the menacing weasels chasing him in the snow – his mother crying – Mordecia smiling at him. Then with sheer determination to survive, he snapped back to reality and to Steilwater the alligator that was only a few feet from him! *"NO! I won't give up!"* Steilwater was closer; Dutch-Henry kicked, twisted, and turned in the water until he was able to pull his backpack off as the alligator opened his huge mouth extremely wide! It was very noticeable that the rabbit was totally exhausted and fatigued from the lack of air. Nevertheless, he managed to push his backpack into the alligator's open mouth as it closed down with tremendous force! *SNAPPP!* Steilwater, the monster alligator twisted and turned his large body to tear the blue backpack into pieces! Air bubbles swirled everywhere – and it was through this confusion Dutch-Henry was able to escape! Dutch-Henry's head finally erupted up from beneath the water! He gasped uncontrollable for air! He coughed and quickly swam to the safety of land. Yolandor helped the wet and tired Dutch-Henry from the water. As she pulled the exhausted rabbit from the water, she fell when her wet paw slipped off Dutch-Henry's. He fell next to her breathing hard. They both turned their heads back to the lagoon and waited. It was now Mordecia's turn to come out of the water that held death –

"There!" shouted, Yolandor! "There's Mordecia!" It was the frog swimming desperately with his jaws puffed out and one arm wrapped around an old rusty box nearly twice his size! Mordecia submerged under the murky water as Steilwater surfaced! There was nothing Yolandor nor Dutch-Henry could do! They just stood in awe of the situation! The frog's head broke through the water and

 Steilwater submerged! Dutch-Henry with a heartfelt enthusiasm cheered his friend on. "Hurry, Mordecia,

hurry!" The frog's tiny little arms and body were trying, but to no avail! The box was slowing him down too much and the alligator was now getting ready to strike! And he did! *CHOMP!!! - SPLAS-H-H!* He missed! Yolandor fainted! Dutch-Henry moved closer to the water! Suddenly it began to rain extremely hard as Mordecia still struggled to make it to shore! Steilwater slid so smoothly through the water and rain! Once again with his great speed he over powered the helpless frog as he closed in! The rain made it almost impossible to see what was going! Huge droplets of water bounced off Dutch-Henry's face as he nervously moved closer to the lagoon! "No-o-o-o," he shouted as he hurriedly hopped toward the water! Steilwater had reached Mordecia with his mouth wide opened! When surprisingly, with all his might, Dutch-Henry mightily hopped from the land toward the alligator! As Steilwater's mouth began to closed, Dutch-Henry landed dead center onto Steilwater's long broad mouth and forced them closed! Yes! He knocked Steilwater's face back into the water! Following that, Dutch-Henry had enough momentum and strength to bounce off Steilwater somersaulting sideways out of control toward a tree branch that hung over the lagoon!

"Gotta!" shouted the rabbit as he grabbed the branch! The large branch began to bend and immediately flung Dutch-Henry to shore! The water below him exploded with great fury! The great Steilwater snapped the tree branch in half. Meanwhile, Dutch-Henry picked himself up off the wet grass as the rain continued to pour down. He heard a familiar voice. "Dutch-Henry, you were superb; just simply, superb!" It was Mordecia who through Dutch-Henry's heroic effort was granted enough time to get to land. Yolandor was behind the frog with a smile and with the box that they all had worked so hard to get. The rain fell a little harder. Mordecia and Yolandor definitely saw a change in Dutch-Henry. He seemed so composed, more self-controlled. She excitably gave him the rusty box. Dutch-Henry wiped some of the water from his eyes. He fumbled with the latch and slowly opened the box. His eyes widened and –

"Nothing – There's nothing in this box!" Yolandor and Mordecia moved closer to take a peek for themselves. Mordecia look at Dutch-Henry,

"Yeah, there is nothing in there. You think Steilwater opened it and still has whatever was in the box?"

"There never was anything in the box," answered, Yolandor. She blushed – "There's usually never is." She tried to smile as she shrugged her shoulders. Dutch-Henry bewildered and not understanding; "What do you mean there usually never is? All my hardships, my struggling, my learning, m-m-my. . ." His voice became calm. He took a long and slow deep breath; "Do all rabbits come of age this way?"

"No." replied, Yolandor. "Some of them don't make it this far. They give up or usually perish in the wilderness. You see, Dutch-Henry, nothing is ever easy and nothing is ever hard. It's just survival and the attitude you put forward to survive. You'll go far in this world; really, you will."

"But, the box – why wasn't something in the box?" Dutch-Henry closed the box to keep the rain out as he looked at Yolandor.

"Just what did you expect to find? Just what?" Dutch-Henry looked at Mordecia for the answer – then looked back at Yolandor – "Something, I risk my life to get down here, I risk . . ."

"I-I-I, - Dutch-Henry, don't you realize what you have achieved?" interrupted, Mordecia. "Dutchie, welcome to the world of life – there need not be anything in that box. There are gifts, there are rewards, and sometime there are painful experiences. And I'm very sure that in time you will realize the many rewards of life." He slowly showed the rabbit his old familiar smile.

The rain finally stopped as the sun unsuccessfully tried to break through the gray clouds. Dutch-Henry glanced at the lagoon and saw his demolished blue

backpack float away. He sighed.

It was three days later; Dutch-Henry sat atop a small hill that overlooked the lagoon. Mordecia and Yolandor were there at his side. He sat there in splendor and thought about all things he had learned and what his journey back home might be like. He adjusted his new blue backpack, smiled at his two friends. There were no words to describe his appreciation and his devoted love for them. He stared at the water ~ "You know, I wonder if Steilwater still runs deep?" He laughed! Yolandor jokingly slapped his backpack and Mordecia had the last words – "Oh, yeah, the lad has come of age with jokes like that." Then they all laughed their way off the hill.

. . . . and somewhere out there, another rabbit is preparing to leave the securities of home to come of age.

The end.

For more adventures of Mordecia; add Mirabella
to your collections of books by artist and writer
Edwin Gilven...